Jet Pack Power

by Jonny Zucker

Illustrated by Mark Penman

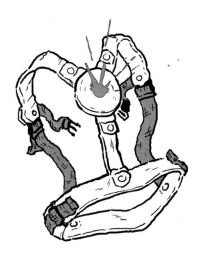

FULL FLI

Titles in Full Flight Gripping Stories

Midsummer Mutants	David Orme
Beekeeper	Danny Pearson
Labyrinth	Melanie Joyce
The Incredible Save	Alison Hawes
Sci-Fi Spy Guy	Roger Hurn
Ghost Camp	Jillian Powell
Stone Beasts	Richard Taylor
Alien Speed Smash	Jonny Zucker
Jet Pack Power	Jonny Zucker
Hero: A War Dog's Tale	Jane A C West

Badger Publishing Limited
Oldmedow Road,
Hardwick Industrial Estate,
King's Lynn PE30 4JJ
Telephone: 01438 791037
www.badgerlearning.co.uk

2 4 6 8 10 9 7 5 3 1

Jet Pack Power ISBN 978 1 84926 265 1

Badger Publishing would like to thank Jonny Zucker
for his help in putting this series together.

Publisher: David Jamieson
Editor: Danny Pearson
Design: Fiona Grant
Illustration: Mark Penman

Contents

New words:

inventor	invention
jealous	stolen
judder	incredibly
microchips	permission

Characters:

Sky

Jed

Mac

Chris

Chapter 1
Ultra 1 Jet Pack

Mac lived with his older brother Sky.

Their house was by the sea.

They were very into water sports and were both great surfboarders. Sky was also an amazing inventor.

He'd already won loads of prizes.

But his greatest invention was the Ultra 1 Jet Pack. He'd just finished it.

Other people had invented jet packs before but Sky's was the smallest ever.

It was the size of a CD. It was silver with a red beam of light in the middle.

When you strapped it to your back you could fly for over an hour. And you could travel at speeds of up to 70 miles per hour.

The last two nights he'd been out testing it. Mac badly wanted to try it out for himself.

"Can I have a go?" he asked Sky on Sunday night.

Sky shook his head. "I still need to check out a few things before anyone else uses it."

"Please!" begged Mac.

"Sorry mate," replied Sky, "but it's no."

That night Mac waited until Sky had gone to bed. Fifteen minutes later he crept downstairs. The Ultra 1 was on the table in Sky's lab. Mac picked it up and stepped out of the house.

The sky was black with a deep cover of stars. He strapped the Ultra 1 onto his back and flicked the 'ON' switch. The jet pack powered up with almost no sound.

A few seconds later, Mac felt a judder
on his back and he was shot up into the
night sky.

Chapter 2

Fly Time

Mac sped upwards and then swooped down. He flew low over the sea. It was amazing. He was really flying!

He tried all sorts of moves - spinning, twisting, speeding up and slowing down. He almost forgot to check his watch. But when he did he saw that he had been out for nearly an hour.

He turned back and headed home.

Inside the house he put the jet pack exactly where he'd found it and went to bed.

Next day in school, Jed and Kris came up to Mac. Jed and Kris were really annoying. They were jealous of Mac because he had an inventor for a brother.

"What new invention is Sky working on?" asked Jed.

"I don't know," replied Mac.

"Liar!" snapped Kris. "Tell us now!"

"Forget it!" shouted Mac.

He walked away.

"We will find out ourselves!" called Jed.

That night when Sky was in bed, Mac tried out the Ultra 1 again. This time he flew higher and faster. It was brilliant!

In school on Tuesday, Jed and Kris grabbed Mac by the arm.

"We know what Sky's new invention is!" said Jed.

"Oh yeah?" replied Mac.

"We were on the pier and we saw you with that jet pack," said Kris.

Jed and Kris were always hanging out by the flagpole on the pier.
Mac's heart sank.

"We want a go on it!" said Jed.

"Forget it!" snapped Mac.

"No," said Kris, shoving his face into Mac's. "We will not forget it. We want to try it out on Friday night."

"Well you can't!" shouted Mac.

He pulled away from them and ran off
down the corridor.

That night he had another go on the
Ultra 1. This time he flew very high
over the town. He knew it was a mad
thing to do because if anyone saw him
they would probably call the police. But
no one did see him.

When he got home though, he could
not sleep. All he could think about was
Jed and Kris. Why wouldn't they just
leave him alone?

Chapter 3
Bad Luck

At break time on Wednesday, Mac went to his locker. The lock had been broken and all of his stuff had been chucked on the floor.

Jed and Kris were standing nearby laughing at him. Mac picked his stuff up and tried to ignore them. But he was very angry.

At lunchtime he went to get his PE kit from the back of his bike. The front tyre of the bike was gone. Jed and Kris were looking at him out of a window, laughing at him.

"Bad luck!" yelled Jed.

"Give me back my tyre!" shouted Mac.

"Sorry!" laughed Kris. "You only get it back when you let us try out the jet pack!"

"I told you!" snapped Mac. "You can't have a go!"

If Wednesday had been bad, Thursday was even worse.

First Mac couldn't find his trainers, then he saw a huge hole in his maths book and at the end of the day, he found his school bag had been glued together so he couldn't open it.

"This is good stuff," smiled Kris as he and Jed walked up to Mac. Kris was holding a tube of glue. It was the brand new glue that Sky had invented. They must have stolen it from Sky's lab!

"Hey give that back and leave me alone!" yelled Mac, snatching the glue off Kris and stuffing it in his jacket pocket.

"We will leave you alone if you let us try out the jet pack tomorrow night," said Kris.

"I told you already!" shouted Mac. "FORGET IT!"

That night, Sky asked Mac, "have you seen that new glue I invented?"

Mac went red in the face. He felt the glue in his jacket pocket. Should he tell Sky about Kris and Jed? Half of him wanted to, but the other half said no. Telling Sky might just make things worse.

"No I haven't," replied Mac.

That night, Mac was in such a bad mood that he did not go out with the Ultra 1. He was worried about Kris and Jed. But he was also worried about Sky.

If Sky found out he'd been using the Ultra 1 he'd kill him.

Would Jed and Kris really tell him?

Chapter 4

Human Bullet

On Friday in school, Jed and Kris stayed well out of Mac's way. There was no shouting or laughing or dirty tricks. Mac was very pleased. Maybe they had just forgotten about him?

That night, after Sky had gone to bed, Mac crept out of the house again with the Ultra 1.

He flew incredibly fast - like a human bullet. He flew so low over the sea that his hands brushed the top of the water.

He went much further than he'd been before; a good two or three miles out to sea. He had just turned back for home, when he suddenly heard a clicking noise.

It only lasted a few seconds and then stopped.

It's nothing, he told himself. Don't worry.

But then the clicking noise sounded even louder. Mac suddenly felt a judder on his back. Sparks shot out of the Ultra 1.

A split second later, the jet pack lost all power.

"NOOOOO!" screamed Mac as he crashed down towards the sea.

Chapter 5

Sky's Glue

Mac's body was about to hit the waves when suddenly he felt something being stuck onto his back and he was lifted up into the air.

He spun round.

It was Sky!

"H...h...how did you get here?" shouted Mac.
"I have the Ultra 1."

"I have invented two even smaller ones," replied Sky.

"The Ultra 2 and the Ultra 3. They are the size of microchips. I have one on, you have the other."

"But how did you know I was here?" asked Mac.

"When I went down to get a drink tonight, I saw the Ultra 1 was gone and I spotted Jed and Kris running away from the house. I realised you must be trying it out and that maybe they had messed about without it. I was right on both counts, wasn't I? So I sped out to sea. It's lucky I found you!"

"Will you kill me for trying out the Ultra 1?" asked Mac as they sped above the water.

"No," replied Sky, "but NEVER do anything like this again. You could have died out here."

They were near home and Sky was beginning to nose dive, when Mac called out to him.

"There is one more thing to do tonight!"

He quickly explained his plan to Sky.

They swooped low over the beach and onto the pier. Jed and Kris were standing by the flagpole, looking out to sea, with their backs facing Mac and Sky.

"YOU COULD HAVE KILLED MY BROTHER!" yelled Sky swooping down towards them.

They spun round and frooze with fear.

"It was only a joke!" they cried.

"Killing someone isn't funny," snapped Sky.

"But this will be!" shouted Mac.

Mac pulled Sky's glue out of his jacket pocket and quickly poured some onto Jed and Kris's backs.

Then Mac grabbed Kris and Sky grabbed Jed.

They swooped up over the pier until they reached the flagpole. Then they stuck Jed and Kris to the top of it.

"HEY!" screamed Kris, "YOU CAN'T
LEAVE US HERE!"

"YES WE CAN!" laughed Mac, as he and Sky headed off for home.

Jed and Kris spent a very long and very cold night on the pier.

Mac didn't try out the Ultra 1 again. He was too busy testing out the Ultra 2 and the Ultra 3 - with Sky's permission of course. And he couldn't wait for the Ultra 4. Sky was working on it and it would be ready very soon.

Jet Packs

For thousands of years, human beings have wanted to fly. The Greek myth of Icarus is about a boy who flew too near to the Sun.

Jet packs were first written about in the 1920's, but this was only in science fiction books.

In the 1960's scientists began working on the first real jet packs. These were powered by jets of escaping gas. They could only fly very short distances.

Astronauts have sometimes used jet packs when re-entering the Earth's orbit after going to space.

Jet packs can't fly very high because of air pressure and zero gravity.

The most famous jet pack flyer is Yves Rossy. He built the jet wingpack. It cost $190,000 to make.

In May 2004, Rossy made a 6 minute flight near Lake Geneva in Switzerland.

In September 2008, Rossy flew over the English Channel. He made the trip in 9 minutes and 7 seconds. He travelled at speeds of up to 186 miles per hour.

Questions

- *Where did Mac find the Ultra 1?*

- *How did Jed and Kris find out about the Ultra 1?*

- *When did Jed and Kris want to try out the Ultra 1?*

- *What was the first mean thing Jed and Kris did to Mac?*

- *How did Mac know that the Ultra 1 was going wrong?*

- *Why did Mac stop Sky from going straight home after he had been rescued?*